THE WEATHER'S BET

ED YOUNG

words by Stephen Cowan

 PHILOMEL BOOKS

The symbols used in this story for the heavenly elements are based on seal characters of Chinese pictograms.

The current of the wind power is drawn ᾇ with a line inside ᾇ to denote the eye of a storm and the micro life-forms it carries. ᾇ

The vertical line of the rain power is the rising sea air ᅮ touching the cooler atmosphere ᾏ above, forming a cloud which condenses and falls in drops as rain. ᾏ

The circle is the sun power with a line in the center to show its energy emitted from within. ⊝

The first two powers, wind and rain, are used in China often to describe "troubled times." That notion inspired the retelling of this timeless classic tale as a reminder that our endangered, vulnerable planet must be sustained by respect.

PHILOMEL BOOKS
An imprint of Penguin Random House LLC, New York

First published in the United States of America by Philomel Books, an imprint of Penguin Random House LLC, 2020.

Visit us online at penguinrandomhouse.com

LIBRARY OF CONGRESS CATALOGING-IN-PUBLICATION DATA
Names: Young, Ed, author, illustrator. | Hudak, John (Photographer), illustrator.
Title: The weather's bet / Ed Young ; photography, John Hudak. Description: New York : Philomel Books, 2020. | Audience: Ages 4–8. | Audience: Grades 2–3. | Summary: Retells the fable, "The Wind and the Sun," in which Wind, Rain, and Sun attempt to remove the cap of a shepherdess. Collage illustrations include symbols based on seal characters of Chinese pictograms. Identifiers: LCCN 2019035608 | ISBN 9780525513827 (hardcover) | ISBN 9780525513834 (ebook) | Subjects: CYAC: Winds—Fiction. | Rain and rainfall—Fiction. | Sun—Fiction. | Wagers—Fiction. Classification: LCC PZ7.Y855 We 2020 | DDC {E}—dc23 | LC record available at https://lccn.loc.gov/2019035608

Manufactured in China by RR Donnelley Asia Printing Solutions Ltd.

ISBN 9780525513827
10 9 8 7 6 5 4 3 2 1

Edited by Jill Santopolo.
Text set in P22 Mayflower.
The art was done from torn handmade and magazine paper.

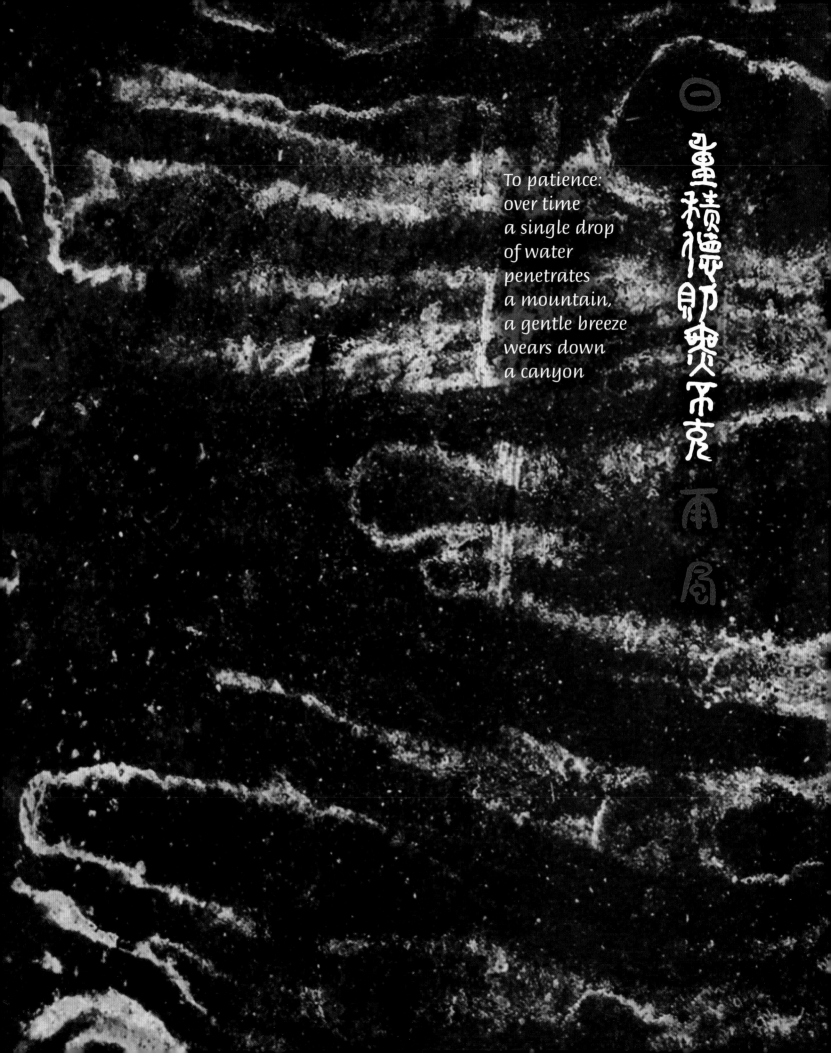

To patience:
over time
a single drop
of water
penetrates
a mountain,
a gentle breeze
wears down
a canyon

Once upon the sky, there were three powers

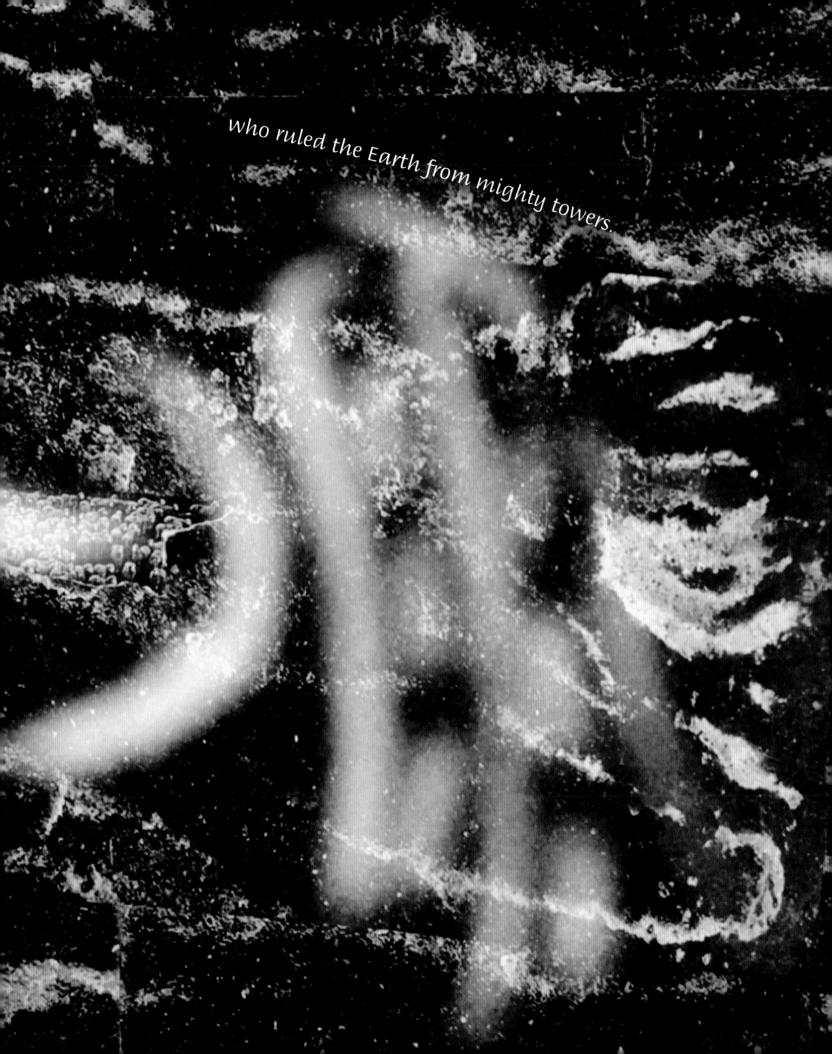

who ruled the Earth from mighty towers.

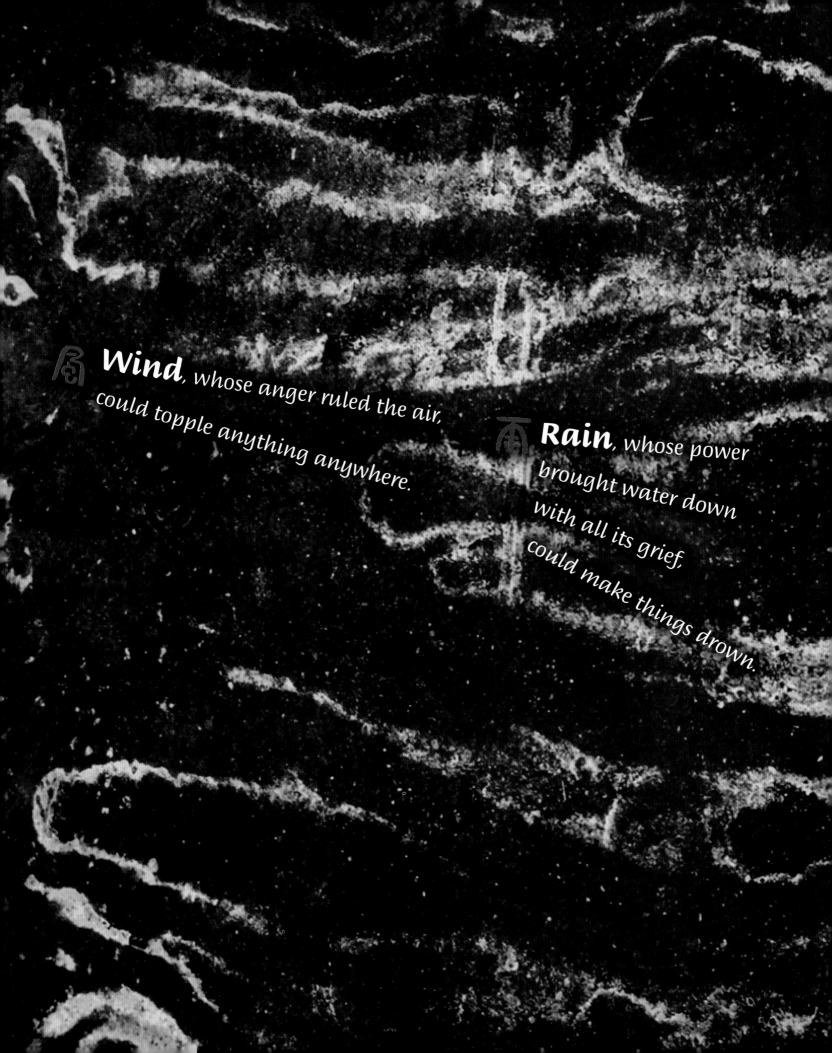

Wind, whose anger ruled the air, could topple anything anywhere.

Rain, whose power brought water down with all its grief, could make things drown.

Sun, whose joy ruled the light, could bring dawn's hope beyond the night.

One day a shepherd was fast asleep

upon a hill with her flock of sheep.

Wind bet, as the shepherd
took her nap,
that it could make her
lose her cap.

Blowing angry gusts of air,

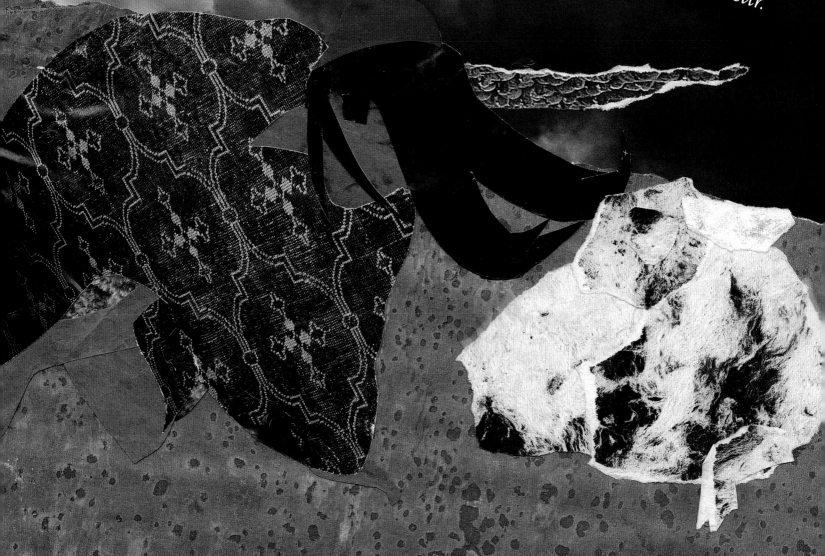

Wind howled and howled

both far and near.

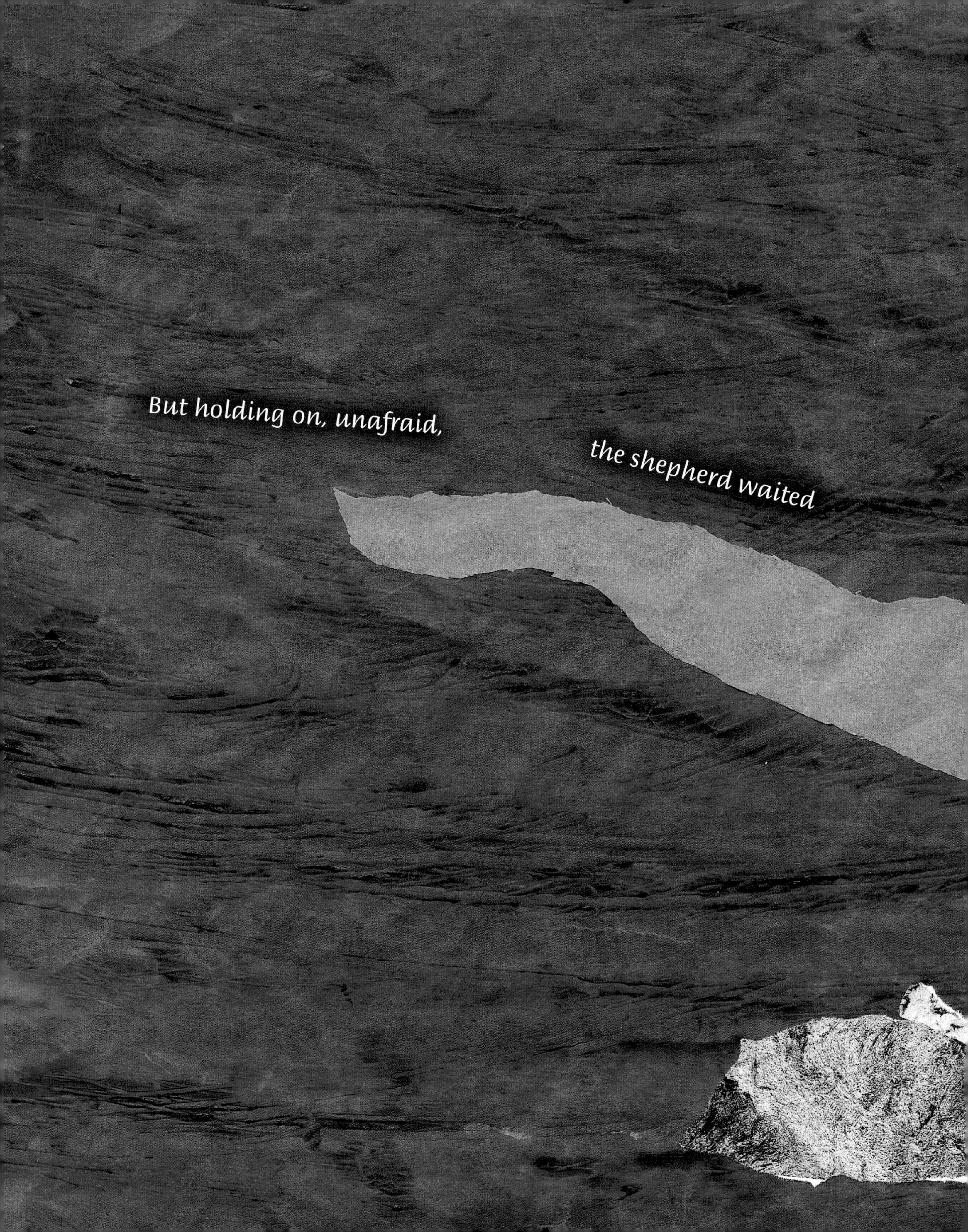

But holding on, unafraid,

the shepherd waited

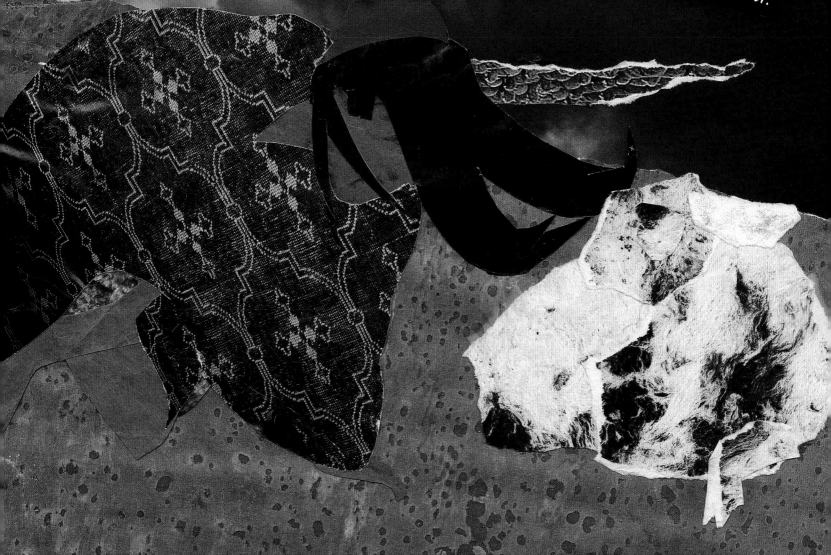

Wind howled and howled

both far and near.

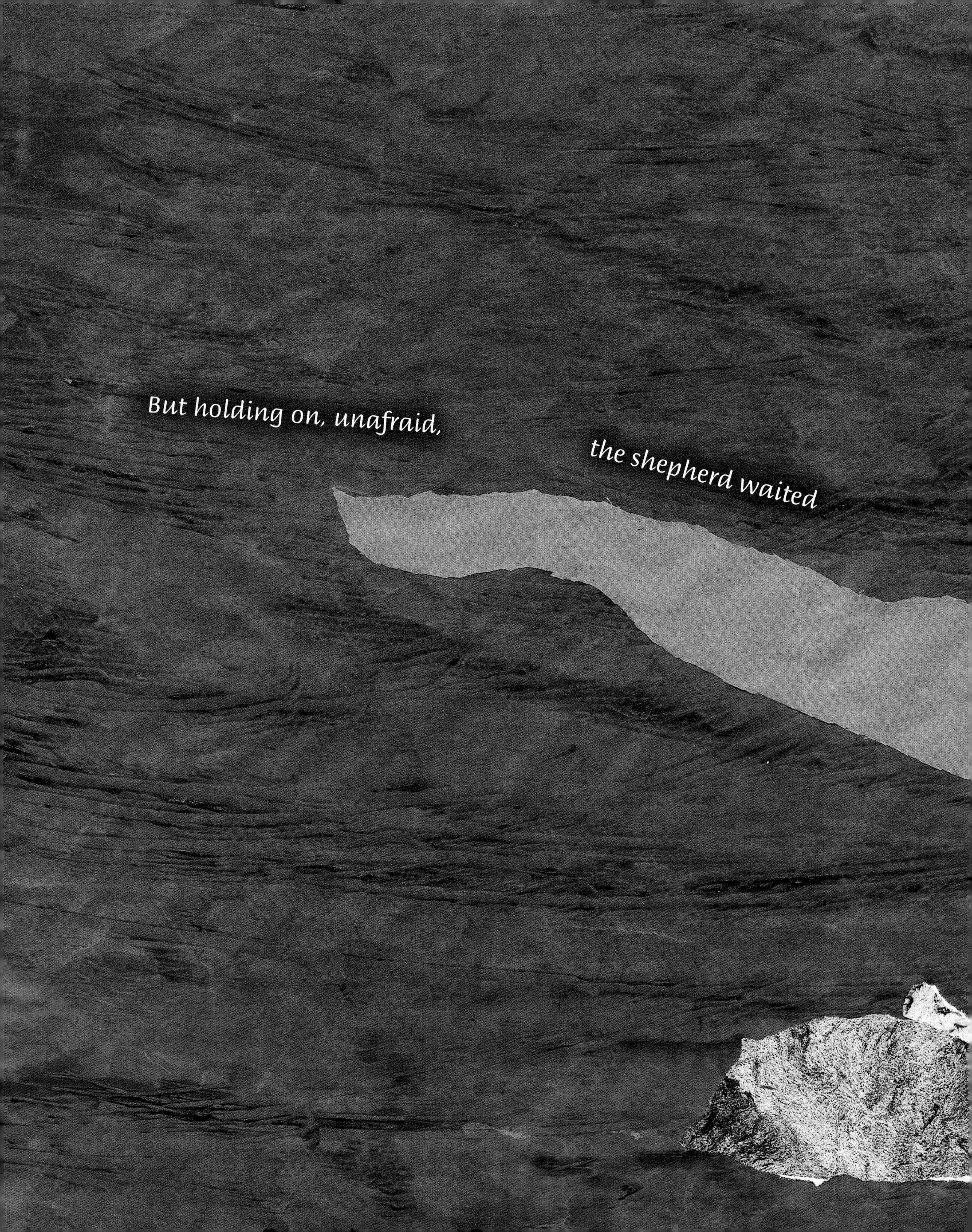

But holding on, unafraid,

the shepherd waited

for the Wind to fade.

Then Rain came down
and tried to soak,

with
pounding
water,

her cap
and
cloak.

Tears
poured
down
and
made
a
flood.

but the shepherd smiled and danced in the mud.

Then behind a cloud

peeked gentle Sun,

whose light beamed down

on everyone.

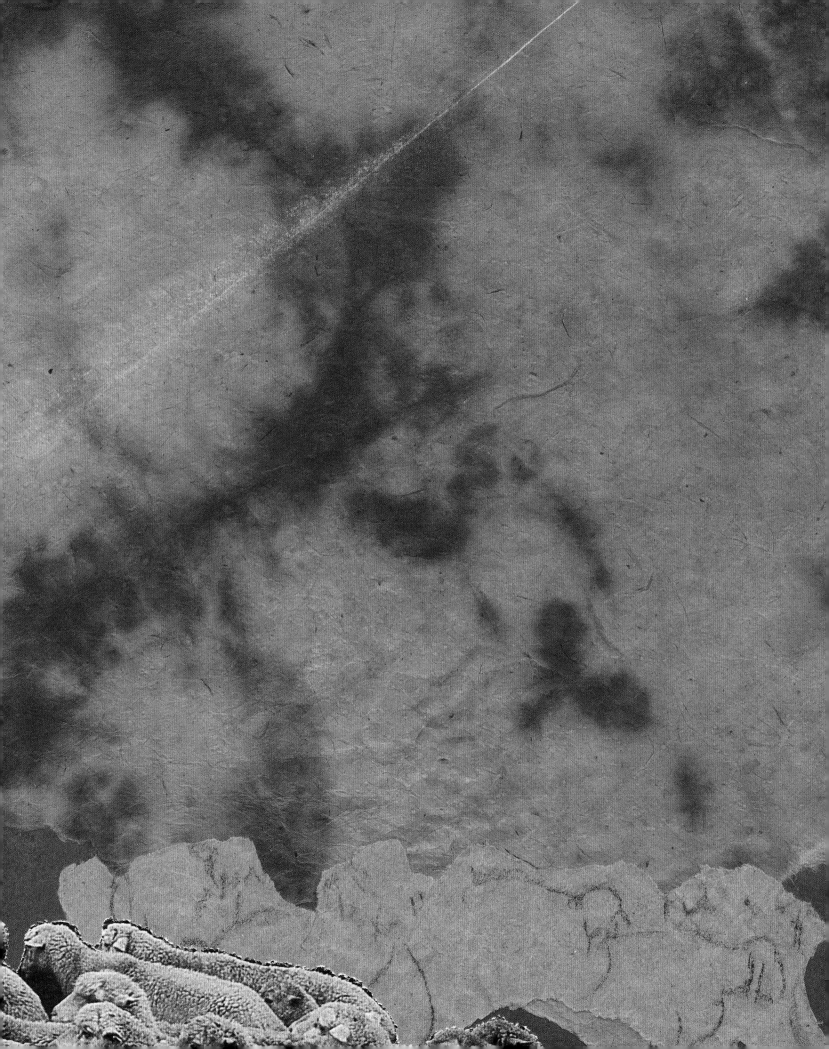

The shepherd smiled and began to sweat, and Wind and Rain lost the bet.

For with the passing morning storm,
She laughed her cap off as she got warm.

風 雨

Wind and Rain then humbly bowed

to the joyful light behind the cloud.

As the three looked down upon the scene,

the hills and valleys all turned green.

And the shepherd

      smiled at the

        setting Sun

          for she knew

       in her heart

that the Earth had won.